ISBN 978-1-78270-512-3

This edition first published 2022

Published by Award Publications Limited,
The Old Riding School, Welbeck, Worksop, S80 3LR

❶ /awardpublications ⓘ @award.books 🐦 @award_books
www.awardpublications.co.uk

22-1035 1

Printed in China

Ready Steady Readers

The Great Big Enormous Turnip

Retold by Sophie Giles

Illustrated by Lawrie Taylor

award

Once upon a time, a little old man and a little old woman lived in a pretty cottage with a great big garden. He grew wonderful vegetables, which she made into delicious stews and pies.

Early one spring morning, the little old man went into the garden to plant some turnip seeds. He dug a shallow trench, scattered a few seeds along it, and carefully covered them with soil.

Then he watered the soil, put his tools away and went to make a cup of tea.

After a few weeks, little green shoots began to poke out of the ground. The little old man carefully hoed around the young plants to make sure there were no weeds or stones in their way.

The young turnips grew and grew. But one of them grew much faster than the others.

Every day, the little old man watched in amazement as the turnip grew bigger and bigger and bigger.

The turnip grew and grew.
At first, it was the size of a football.

Then it was the size of a barrel.
And then it was as large as the wheelbarrow.

And still it grew and grew, until it became
a great big enormous turnip, the size of the
little old man's favourite armchair.

The little old man looked at the great big enormous turnip. "How wonderful!" he said.

The little old woman looked at the great big enormous turnip. "How will it ever fit into my cooking pot?" she asked.

One morning, the little old woman said,
"Why don't you dig up that turnip today so
I can make us a nice stew for dinner?"

Now, the little old man didn't really want to pull up the great big enormous turnip. But, taking his garden fork, he went to dig it up as the little old woman had asked.

The little old man dug all around the turnip to loosen the soil. Then he grasped it firmly, and pulled. And pulled...

But the great big enormous turnip wouldn't budge.

"My goodness," said the little old man. "I shall need some help with this." And he called to the little old woman.

The little old woman held the little old man around his waist. The little old man grasped the great big enormous turnip, and together they pulled. And they pulled...

But the great big enormous turnip wouldn't budge.

"My goodness!" said the little old woman. "We'll need some help with this." And she called the boy from next door.

The boy next door came and held the little old woman around her waist. The little old woman held the little old man around his waist, and the little old man grasped the great big enormous turnip.

Together they pulled. And they pulled...

But the great big enormous turnip wouldn't budge.

"We need some more help with this," said the boy from next door. And he called his sister.

The girl from next door held her brother around his waist. The boy held the little old woman around her waist. The little old woman held the little old man around his waist, and the little old man grasped the great big enormous turnip.

Together they pulled. And they pulled...

But the great big enormous turnip wouldn't budge.
"We need some more help with this," said the girl
from next door, and she called the dog.

The dog held on to the girl. The girl held on
to the boy. The boy held on to the little old woman.
The little old woman held on to the little old man,
and the little old man grasped the great big
enormous turnip.

Together they pulled. And they pulled...
But the great big enormous turnip wouldn't budge.
"We need some more help with this," woofed the
dog, and he called the cat.

The cat held on to the dog. The dog held on to the girl. The girl held on to the boy. The boy held on to the little old woman. The little old woman held on to the little old man, and the little old man grasped the great big enormous turnip.

Together they pulled. And they pulled...

But the great big enormous turnip still
wouldn't budge.

"We need some more help with this,"
miaowed the cat, and she called the mouse.

The mouse held on to the cat. The cat held on to the dog. The dog held on to the girl. The girl held on to the boy. The boy held on to the little old woman. The little old woman held on to the little old man, and the little old man grasped the great big enormous turnip.

Together they pulled. And pulled...

And, *at last*, the great big enormous turnip began to move.

sshlllluuuuppp!

The little old man, the little old woman, the boy from next door, the girl from next door, the dog, the cat and the mouse all tumbled to the ground as the turnip came out of the ground with a great big enormous **sshlllluuuuppp!**

That evening, the little old man, the little old woman, the boy and the girl, the dog, the cat and the mouse all sat down together at the table and filled their plates with the most delicious turnip stew they had ever tasted!

Are you a
Ready Steady Readers
SUPERSTAR?

gr   ou

a_e   ew

Key sounds

Race to point to the words in the story that use these key sounds.

OR

Clap each time you hear one used as the story is read aloud.

Different voices

Think about how you could use different voices to show how the characters feel.

My goodness!

How will it ever fit into my cooking pot?

We need some more help with this.

Look, find, count and talk!

Can you **find** this mouse somewhere in the book?

Go back through the story. How many blue birds can you **count**?

The turnip was delicious. What **other words** do you know that can mean delicious?

Look back at page 11.

Why do you think the little old man didn't want to dig up the great big enormous turnip?

Notes for Grown-Ups

Ready Steady Readers build young readers' vocabulary, develop their comprehension skills and boost their progress towards independent reading.

Research carried out by BookTrust has found that children who are regularly read to, or with, have stronger bonds with their family members, a more positive sense of self, greater well-being and improved educational outcomes, health and creativity.

★ Make storytime fun to grow a love of reading. Build it into your regular routine, whether you're reading aloud, listening to your child read, or reading separate books together. Why not create a special reading space? It could be as elaborate as a decorated den, or as simple as a special cushion on the floor.

★ Be a Reading Role Model: if your child sees you read, they will copy. So let them 'catch' you reading and enjoying a range of books and magazines. Reading opportunities are everywhere, and the key is enjoyment.

★ Encourage your child to read aloud to help pick up and resolve any difficulties they might have. As their skills grow, it will also help their fluency and expression. For older children, 'reading in their head' is an important skill to learn, though reading aloud regularly will help to develop their overall confidence.

★ Work through the activities at the back of the book with your child to help them develop their observation, comprehension and communication skills.

★ Always keep a positive attitude and focus on your child's achievements. You could say, "You found that word tricky, but you kept trying! Well done!" This will boost their confidence and grow their enjoyment of reading.